Be Who You Were Meant To Be

written by
Lauren Grabois Fischer

illustrated by
Devin Hunt

The Be Books

www.TheBEbooks.com

I hope that you enjoy this book and the fun activities that follow after. If you come up with a great activity that promotes kindness, positivity, and love, and you want to share it with me, you can email your ideas to lauren@thebebooks.com or find me on social media @thebebooks!

You can follow my page for positive posts, updates on book giveaways, and new books coming out. I would love to share your beautiful creations with others. You can have your parents post them on social media and tag **@thebebooks**. Make sure to use **#thebebooks**, **#laurengraboisfischer**, and **#bethelightbethechange** in your posts.

ISBN: 978-0-9862532-0-1

www.TheBEbooks.com
@theBEbooks

This book is dedicated to my sisters, Candice, Jackie, and Danielle. I am so
thankful to have them in my life. I have been blessed with many angels in my life,
and my sisters are three of them. What a blessing to share life with three people
that just "get me" and know me completely and love me just as I am. Our deep
connections, understanding of each other, and closeness is always inspiring to
me and helps me "be me" in this great big world. I am here for you forever and
always, and I am so thankful that we have each other.

I also want to dedicate this book to all of the people who stay true to themselves; to
all of the hard-workers and dreamers, to all of you who know who you are and
are proud to show the world. Stand tall. Speak proudly.

You are amazing... Just as you are!

You were born to be unique

To stand out in a crowd

Show the world what you
are made of

Stand
tall
and
be
proud

It is okay to be different

In fact it is the best thing to be

Be who you are
No need for conformity

We are all special and unique

We all have so much to share

Learn
your special
talents

Know just
what makes
you who
you are

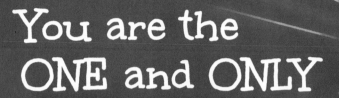

You are the
ONE and ONLY

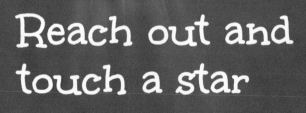

Reach out and
touch a star

Be positive, brave and confident

Make the best of each day

Be grateful and kind always

Find time for silence and prayer

Plan ahead and dream big

You can go anywhere

Remain who you are

As you grow and succeed

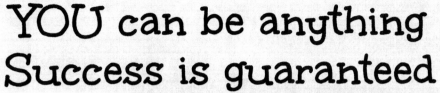

YOU can be anything
Success is guaranteed

Sé Quien Quieres Ser

Escrito por

Lauren Grabois Fischer

Ilustrado por

Devin Hunt

Naciste para ser único y

Sobresalir entre la multitud

Está bien ser diferente

De hecho es mejor ser así

Sé quien eres y no te conformes

Somos todos especiales y únicos

Tenemos todos muchas cosas que compartir

Ponlo al universo
Esté atento con ojos
brillantes

Aprende
de tus
talentos
especiales y

Reconoce
que te hace
ser quien tu
eres

ÉRES
ÚNICO

Mira hacia
afuera y alcanza
las estrellas

Sea positiva, valiente y

Haz lo mejor de cada día

Sé siempre amable y agradecido

Encuentra tiempo para el silencio y la oración

Sigue siendo quien eres

Crece y sea exitoso

Tu puedes ser lo que quieras el triunfo esta asegurado

Inspiration & Discussion

Dear Parents and Educators,

"Be Who You Were Meant To Be" is a book that I hold very close to my heart. It is and always will be my very first published book. I wrote these words as a poem for my son when he was a baby. It was my wish that as a mom, my son would always know that he is special and different and that the world is ready for his greatness. It is our job as parents and educators to guide our children and students towards positivity, understanding, acceptance, kindness, and love. It is up to us to teach them about humanity and that the world is a beautiful place because we are all different. It is our differences that make us stand out in a crowd and give us purpose in our lives. When each of us can understand this concept, the world will be a very different place. Let us create that world. Let us imagine and build a world with more love than hate, more kindness than pain, more friends than enemies, and more positivity than negativity. We are all children of the world. Every single one of us is different and beautiful just as we are.

On the following pages, you will find discussion questions that can inspire and guide a conversation in your home or classroom. I feel that my purpose is to encourage these dialogues and hope that through deep discussion, every child can become aware of their potential to improve this world. We each have the ability to make a positive influence. It is my hope that through reading my books, and having the proper discussions, every child can go out into the world with confidence, kindness, respect, and positivity.

With love and gratitude,

Lauren Grabois Fischer

- The children on the cover of this book come from all different backgrounds. Why do you think that I chose to have children different than each other rather than putting a group of children that come from the same background? Do you think I did this intentionally?

- This book is my only book that is bilingual. Bilingual means that it comes in more than one language. I chose to write this book in English and Spanish because of my Cuban heritage. Where is your family from? Ask your parents and grandparents about your family history. Find out where your grandparents were born and where they grew up. Find out about your great grandparents. It is a wonderful thing to be educated and to know your own family history.

- I use the word "unique" a couple of times in this book. I wanted you as the reader to ask what this word means. Take the time to ask a parent or teacher what "unique" means. Try using it in a sentence. If you already know what it means, take out a sheet of paper and write a sentence using the word sharing how you are unique. Be yourself and be true to who you are.

- The boy on the first page is standing in the spotlight. Look at the other children surrounding him. Do they look sad or happy that he is in the spotlight? Are they cheering him on or jealous of the attention that he is getting? Talk with a partner about this. It is important that we cheer each other on and be supportive to everyone.

· This book has two different animals in it. Find the animals. Why did I include animals in a book about being yourself? Is it important to show respect to animals as well as humans? Why should we show them respect? How can we show animals respect?

· I use the word "conformity" in this book. What does that mean? When is it okay to conform? When is it okay to change who you are to fit in? Should we have to change to fit into a group? Or should the group accept me for who I am? There is a balance to this. We must be kind, respectful, and peaceful to all people, and if you are doing this, then you should not have to change for others.

· Why is it important to share with others? There are two children playing with the same toy on a page in this book. Why do you think I put an emphasis on this? Do you think that sharing can create a peaceful environment and make others happy?

· I use the words, "Put that out into the universe," in this book. I am a big believer in sharing and spreading more positive energy to others. How can we do this? How can we make this world brighter?

· What is your special talent? What can you contribute to your family, to your classroom, to the world?

· Dream big. Reach out and touch the stars! Make sure that you are living your dreams and creating a world around you that is beautiful and bright. What are your dreams? What do you want to see in this world?

· Be positive, brave and confident... Make the best of each day." That girl is looking out at the rainy day, and all she sees is the rainbow. There will always be "rainy days" in our lives, and things that may not go as planned, but it is important that we focus on the rainbows and the beauty that surrounds us. What are you grateful for? What makes you smile? What makes you happy?

· You can be anything! Study hard. Go to school. Listen to your teachers. Imagine and create the life that you want. It can be yours.

Activity Pages

· Take out a hand held mirror. Look at
your reflection and smile. How does that
make you feel to see your big smile?
Look at your reflection and show sadness.
How does that make you feel? There is
a boy looking at his reflection in this book
and smiling back at himself. What would the
boy see in the mirror if he was sad? What would
he see in the mirror if he was angry? It is important
that we realize that our facial expressions and moods can
affect others, and the world can be like a mirror. It reflects back to
us what we give to others. Smile at others, and you will see that they will
smile back at you. Be kind with your words and actions, and you will get
kindness back in return.

· Create a list of careers that you can see for yourself. The list does not have to be limited to five career paths. Fill this area in with jobs that you would love to do. What do you want to be when you "grow up?" The great news is that you can change this list as you grow and learn more. You can add to it or you can take away from it. It's your life and your decision. What will you become?

1. _____

2. _____

3. _____

4. _____

5. _____

· What kind of schooling is needed to get you to your dream job? Talk with a parent or teacher about how you can become qualified for that job. Take out a sheet of paper and create a diagram, illustration, or drawing showing the steps that you will take to get there.

· Find a friend, sibling or partner and answer the following questions. It is wonderful to listen and share ideas with friends. You may learn something new that you did not know before.

1. What is your favorite thing to do?

2. What is your favorite book to read?

3. Do you have a special talent?
   If so, what is it?

4. Do you have any pets? If the answer is yes, how do you help take care of them?

5. How are you unique? How are you different from someone else?

6. How can you show that you are a confident person?

· Find a quiet place to sit and relax. You can close your eyes or leave them open. Take time to listen to your breath, and block out all of the noise that usually surrounds you. Find at least a minute a day to do this and calm your mind. You will be very grateful that you took the time to love yourself.

· List four qualities that you have that will make this world a better place.

1. _____

2. _____

3. _____

4. _____

· **Gratitude List:** Use the lines below to write five things that you are grateful for.

1. _____

2. _____

3. _____

4. _____

5. _____

· What are three ways that I can be kind to others?

1. _____

2. _____

3. _____

· Name three things that you love about today.

1. _____

2. _____

3. _____

· Continue the following sentences:

I am happy when ...

I can help others by ...

Today I plan to make the world better by ...

COLOR YOUR WORLD

I hope that after reading this book, you are feeling inspired!

Here is the chance for you to add your own style to your new favorite book!

Using CRAYONS only, fill in the pictures with the colors

that make your heart happy.

I can't wait to see what you have created! Take pictures of your BEAUTIFUL,

UNIQUE, and ONE OF A KIND creations and post it on social media.

Tag **@thebebooks** and I will share YOUR CREATION on my stories!

Do not rip out the pages from this book.

If you want more FREE coloring pages, visit my website

www.thebebooks.com for FREE downloads of all of my COLORING pages.

Thank you for **COLORING OUR WORLD!**

Author's Note

Thank you so much for taking the time to read, "Be Who You Were Meant To Be." I want to thank you personally for reading these words that I believe to be so important. I know in my heart that we are all so special just as we are. We all need to see our own greatness within and we need to be confident and proud of who we are. We are sometimes taught to criticize and judge ourselves and each other. Instead, we need to build each other up and be proud of our successes. We need to encourage each other and support each other. There needs to be more acceptance and less bullying. We need to love our own flaws and learn to work with them. We need to grow and learn every single day. We need to be positive people and be kind and accepting to all. Everyone deserves respect and love. And we must remember to love ourselves as well. Be proud of who you are. Be true to yourself.

I added a special page to this version of "Be Who You Were Meant To Be" that was not in the original printing of this book. "Be grateful and kind always. Find time for silence and prayer... Plan ahead and dream big. You can go anywhere." I have learned through experience how powerful mindfulness, prayer, and meditation is for us. May we each find the time daily to nourish our own souls and bodies, through exercise, taking a moment of silence, and listening to our own inner voice. It will help us filter out anything extra that may block us from being our very best selves. Be you... Always!

With love and gratitude,

Lauren Grabois Fischer

CPSIA information can be obtained
at www.ICGtesting.com
Printed in the USA
BVHW020157250121
598666BV00014B/61

9 780986 253201